Dear Parents and Educators,

Welcome to Penguin Young Readers! As parents and educators, you
know that each child develops at his or her own pace—in terms of
speech, critical thinking, and, of course, reading. Penguin Young
Readers recognizes this fact. As a result, each Penguin Young Readers
book is assigned a traditional easy-to-read level (1–4) as well as a
Guided Reading Level (A–P). Both of these systems will help you choose
the right book for your child. Please refer to the back of each book
for specific leveling information. Penguin Young Readers features
esteemed authors and illustrators, stories about favorite characters,
fascinating nonfiction, and more!

Ladybug Girl
Who Can Play?

LEVEL **1**

GUIDED
READING **C**
LEVEL

This book is perfect for an **Emergent Reader** who:
- can read in a left-to-right and top-to-bottom progression;
- can recognize some beginning and ending letter sounds;
- can use picture clues to help tell the story; and
- can understand the basic plot and sequence of simple stories.

Here are some **activities** you can do during and after reading this book:
- Word Repetition: Reread the story and count how many times you
  read the following words: *play, up, down, one, two, three, four*. On a
  separate sheet of paper, work with the child to write a new sentence for
  each word.
- Make Connections: In this story, Lulu has more fun playing with all her
  friends than she does by herself. When have you had more fun because
  your friends were there to play?

Remember, sharing the love of reading with a child is the best gift
you can give!

—Bonnie Bader, EdM
  Penguin Young Readers program

*Penguin Young Readers are leveled by independent reviewers applying the standards developed by Irene Fountas
and Gay Su Pinnell in *Matching Books to Readers: Using Leveled Books in Guided Reading*, Heinemann, 1999.

PENGUIN YOUNG READERS
Published by the Penguin Group
Penguin Group (USA), 375 Hudson Street, New York, New York 10014, USA

USA | Canada | UK | Ireland | Australia | New Zealand | India | South Africa | China
Penguin Books Ltd, Registered Offices: 80 Strand, London WC2R 0RL, England

For more information about the Penguin Group visit penguin.com

Text copyright © 2013 by Jacky Davis. Illustrations copyright © 2013 by David Soman. All rights reserved. Published by Penguin Young Readers, an imprint of Penguin Group (USA), 345 Hudson Street, New York, New York 10014. Manufactured in China.

Library of Congress Cataloging-in-Publication Data is available.

ISBN 978-0-448-46501-2 (pbk)   10 9 8 7 6 5 4 3 2 1
ISBN 978-0-448-46502-9 (hc)   10 9 8 7 6 5 4 3 2 1

Ladybug Girl

Ladybug Girl is a *New York Times* Best Seller

Who Can Play?

by David Soman and Jacky Davis
illustrated by Les Castellanos

Penguin Young Readers
An Imprint of Penguin Group (USA)

Who can play?

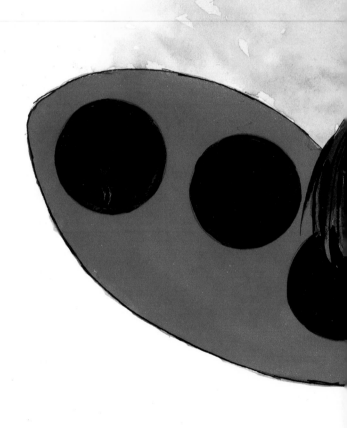

One can play.

7

One can play and play.

One can go up.

One can go down.

One can play and play all day.

But it is not so fun this way.

Who can play?

Two can play.

Two can play and play.

Two can go up.

Two can go down.

Two can play and play all day.

But it is not so fun this way.

Who can play?

Three can play.

Three can play and play.

Three can go up.

Three can go down.

Three can play and play
all day.

But it is not so fun this way.

Who can play?

Four can play.

Four can play and play.

Four can go up.

Four can go down.

Four can play and play
all day.

But it is not so fun this way.

Who can play?

We can play.

We can play and play all day.